P9-CFW-021

WELCOME TO
PASSPORT TO READING
A beginning reader's ticket to a brand-new world!

Every book in this program is designed to build read-along and read-alone skills, level by level, through engaging and enriching stories. As the reader turns each page, he or she will become more confident with new vocabulary, sight words, and comprehension.

These PASSPORT TO READING levels will help you choose the perfect book for every reader.

READING TOGETHER
Read short words in simple sentence structures together to begin a reader's journey.

READING OUT LOUD
Encourage developing readers to sound out words in more complex stories with simple vocabulary.

READING INDEPENDENTLY
Newly independent readers gain confidence reading more complex sentences with higher word counts.

READY TO READ MORE
Readers prepare for chapter books with fewer illustrations and longer paragraphs.

This book features sight words from the educator-supported Dolch Sight Words List. This encourages the reader to recognize commonly used vocabulary words, increasing reading speed and fluency.

For more information, please visit passporttoreadingbooks.com.

Enjoy the journey!

Little, Brown and Company
Hachette Book Group
1290 Avenue of the Americas, New York, NY 10104
Visit us at lb-kids.com
marvelkids.com

First Edition: April 2017

Little, Brown and Company is a division of Hachette Book Group, Inc.
The Little, Brown name and logo are trademarks of Hachette Book Group, Inc.

The publisher is not responsible for websites (or their content) that are
not owned by the publisher.

ISBNs: 978-0-316-27169-1 (pbk.), 978-0-316-43892-6 (Scholastic edition),
978-0-316-55392-6 (ebook), 978-0-316-55390-2 (ebook), 978-0-316-31198-4 (ebook)

Printed in the United States of America

CW

10 9 8 7 6 5 4 3 2 1

Passport to Reading titles are leveled by independent reviewers applying the standards
developed by Irene Fountas and Gay Su Pinnell in *Matching Books to Readers:
Using Leveled Books in Guided Reading*, Heinemann, 1999.

MARVEL

GUARDIANS OF THE GALAXY VOL. 2

THE GUARDIANS SAVE THE DAY

Adapted by R. R. Busse

Illustrations by Ron Lim, Andy Smith,

Andy Troy, and Chris Sotomayor

Based on the Major Motion Picture

Written and Directed by James Gunn

Produced by Kevin Feige, p.g.a.

Ⓛ Ⓑ

LITTLE, BROWN AND COMPANY

New York   Boston

Attention, GUARDIANS OF THE GALAXY fans! Look for these words when you read this book. Can you spot them all?

planet

monster

dance

Milano

These are the Guardians of the Galaxy!

Star-Lord, Gamora, Drax, Rocket, and Groot are great friends. They are heroes who help protect beings on other planets.

The monster is very hungry
and will eat almost anything.
The planet needs the monster to go away.

Peter Quill is called Star-Lord.

He is the leader of the Guardians.

He has a mask that protects him in a fight.

Gamora is a great fighter.
She is very serious,
but always keeps her promises.
She is too serious sometimes,
but she is learning to be nice.
Peter is helping her!

Drax is also a great fighter.
He does not understand jokes.
He is very glad the Guardians
are his friends.

Rocket and Groot are best friends.

Rocket is smart with machines and traps.

Groot is small.

He likes to dance.

Together as a team,
the Guardians are ready to fight!
They put on their gear.

Groot has his own job.

He will battle small pests.

The monster is here!
It is so big!
It has a wide mouth
and very sharp teeth.

The monster also has a lot of arms.
It is very hungry!
It does not have a lot of food
in outer space.

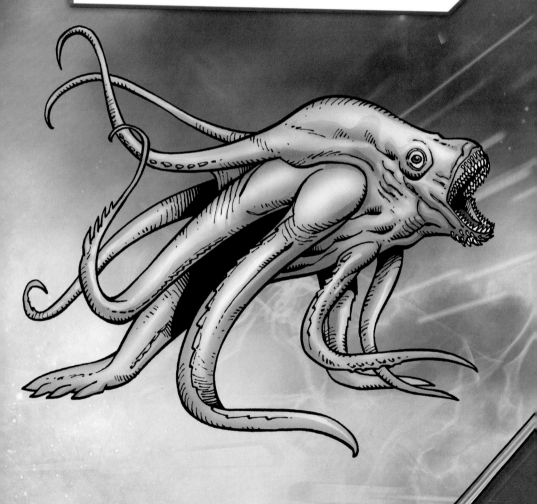

The Guardians are not scared.
They jump in to combat!

They have to save the day
and help Ayesha's planet!
If they lose, beings will be hurt.

Groot listens to Peter's music.
Music makes fighting
the monster fun.

Drax wants to stop the monster fast.
He is angry.

The Guardians try very hard,
but they cannot hurt the monster.
But what is that?

Drax is back!

He fights harder than before.

He is able to help his friends.

The Guardians beat the monster!
Ayesha's planet is safe!

The Guardians are happy!
They are also looking for someone.

It is Nebula, Gamora's sister!
Ayesha caught her stealing.
She is Ayesha's prisoner.

Ayesha thanks Peter and Gamora
for their help.
She is glad her planet is safe.
She sends Nebula with the Guardians.

The Guardians fly off
to another adventure!
Their ship is orange and blue.
It is called the Milano,
and it is very fast.